THE PUPPY PLACE

LOLA

THE PUPPY PLACE

**Don't miss any of these
other stories by Ellen Miles!**

THE PUPPY PLACE

LOLA

ELLEN MILES

SCHOLASTIC INC.

For Scarlett

Copyright © 2016 by Ellen Miles
Cover art by Tim O'Brien
Original cover design by Steve Scott

All rights reserved. Published by Scholastic Inc., *Publishers since 1920*. SCHOLASTIC and associated logos are trademarks and/or registered trademarks of Scholastic Inc.

ISBN 978-1-338-06910-5

10 9 8 7 6 5 4 3 2 1   16 17 18 19 20

Printed in the U.S.A.   40
First printing 2016

CHAPTER ONE

"These rapids look fearsome, Captain Sam!" Charles pointed to the burbling stream that tumbled over brightly-colored pebbles and moss-covered rocks.

"It's nothing we haven't seen before, Captain Charles," said his friend Sammy. "What do you think, Captain David? Can we make it through?"

"Yes, sir," said David, snapping a smart salute. "I scouted it this morning and I believe I found a route we can use. We may make it to the head-waters after all."

The three friends began to wade up the stream, stepping carefully from rock to rock. The bright green moss could be very slippery. They knew that from the day before, when David had fallen in and gotten his jeans and sneakers so wet that they'd had to call off expeditioning for the day.

Expeditioning was the most fun they'd had in a long time. It had all started because of the unit they were doing at school. Charles Peterson and his two best friends were all in room 2B, Mr. Mason's second-grade class. Mr. Mason was the greatest teacher. He was funny and nice and he hardly ever yelled. Plus, he always had something exciting planned for them. This month they were studying explorers.

They had learned about Christopher Columbus, who everybody had already known about ever since preschool, but also about people like Amelia Earhart, an aviator who had flown around the world and then disappeared mysteriously, and

Ernest Shackleton, who had explored the icy world of Antarctica.

All the explorers they studied were amazing, but Charles, David, and Sammy agreed: The most awesome explorers of all time were Lewis and Clark. They had traveled across the American West, mapping a route from St. Louis, Missouri, to the Pacific Ocean and learning about the plants and animals and people who lived along the way. Their group, known as the Corps of Discovery, had boated up rivers and climbed over mountains. They had encountered grizzly bears and bison and had every kind of adventure you could imagine.

When Mr. Mason had divided up the class into teams to do reports on explorers, there had been no question about it: Charles and his friends had picked Lewis and Clark. They had started in right away on their research, and they had already learned a lot.

The expeditioning game had started a week ago, on a sunny, crisp autumn Saturday. They had met at David's house to work on their report. Afterward, they had gone outside to play. "Look," Sammy had said, pointing to the stream that ran along the edge of David's backyard. "It's a mighty river. Should we try to find the headwaters?"

"Headwaters," they had already learned, meant the place where a river began: the smaller streams or springs that added up to a larger flow. The first part of Lewis and Clark's expedition had been to travel up the Missouri River until they found its beginnings.

"It'll be a perilous journey," said Charles, getting right into the game. "We'll need lots of supplies."

"I'm in," said David. "I've always wondered what happens if you go all the way up this stream."

The first day the explorers had traveled only a little way up the stream, along a muddy path that ran along its banks. That part of the "river" was familiar to Charles: He and David had once spent a lot of time in those thick, brambly woods, searching for a scared stray puppy. They had finally caught the scruffy white mutt and taken care of him until they found his family. That puppy, Lucky, had lived up to his name.

Lucky was only one of the puppies Charles and his family had cared for. The Petersons were a foster family who took in puppies who needed help. In Lucky's case, that had meant keeping him until they found out where he belonged. For most of the other puppies, it meant finding them just the right forever families.

Charles's older sister, Lizzie, was crazy about dogs. His younger brother, the Bean, loved them, too. Their mom, a newspaper reporter, was more of a cat person — but fortunately she had a soft spot for puppies. Charles's dad, a firefighter, could never turn away from a person or animal in need. All together, they made a great foster family. It was never easy to say good-bye to the puppies they had cared for, but Charles knew that was how fostering worked. Anyway, they had kept one of them: Buddy, the best puppy ever. He was the cutest, sweetest, most lovable puppy in the whole world, and he was theirs forever.

Now, as he picked his way up the stream, Charles smiled. He was thinking of Buddy and how the little brown mutt would love dashing through these woods. The expeditioners had traveled much further upstream that day, and there was no more muddy path to follow; this time they were in truly unexplored territory. Instead of bright sunshine, there were gloomy gray clouds overhead, but Charles and his friends didn't care about the weather. The courageous explorers were equipped for anything: They carried backpacks with provisions (apples, crackers, chocolate, and a Cub Scout canteen full of water) and plenty of equipment (flashlights, in case they got stuck out after dark, a first aid kit, a compass, and their official expedition journal). If Buddy had been along, he could have worn a backpack, too, carrying his own food and water. Charles decided to bring him on the next expedition.

"Were there any dogs in Lewis and Clark's Corps of Discovery?" he asked Sammy, who was leading that day's march up the stream.

"I don't know, but we can probably find out," said Sammy, pushing through a bramble bush and holding back a branch so that it wouldn't snap into Charles's face.

"I'm sure there weren't any cats," said David. "Slinky never comes anywhere near this stream — I mean, mighty river — if she can help it."

Slinky was David's cat. She was so shy that Charles had only seen her a few times. "How is Slinky, anyway?" Charles asked.

"She's been hiding under my bed a lot lately," David said. "I guess she doesn't like yelling." He bent down to pick up a rock, then stood and tossed it into the stream.

"Who's yelling?" Charles asked.

David shrugged. "My mom and dad. At each other. It's nothing. I think. They just keep getting into arguments lately, ever since my dad lost his job. It's nothing. Never mind." His voice got quieter and quieter until he stopped and bent down for another rock.

Charles and Sammy exchanged looks. David

did not seem happy — but he didn't seem to want to talk about it anymore, either. Charles decided that it was time to change the subject. "Hey, look," he said. "A giant waterfall. We'll have to portage the boats around it. Rally the men, Captain Sam."

The "giant waterfall," actually just a slightly stronger trickle of water over a few rocks, was a good distraction. The boys got busy scouting routes and planning the portage. The expedition's (imaginary) boats would have to be unloaded and carried upstream by some of the (imaginary) explorers while others (also imaginary) lugged the supplies and camping gear that had been packed inside.

"We'll never finish the portage before this storm rolls in," said Sammy, glancing up at the dark clouds that had begun to fill the sky. "Captain Charles, order the men to make camp."

"Yes, sir," said Charles.

"Hey, what's that noise?" Sammy cocked his head, listening.

From far off in the distance came a high-pitched whine. A squeal, really. A sound that tore at Charles's heart. He knew exactly what it was. It was the sound of a dog in trouble.

CHAPTER TWO

"It's an orphaned wolf pup, howling in the wilderness," said Sammy. He was still being Captain Sam.

"Or a coyote," said David. "Or a prairie dog? Do they make noises?"

Charles shook his head. "It's a dog," he said. He wasn't Captain Charles anymore. He was just Charles again. "And it's not a happy dog. We have to find it." Charles couldn't bear the sound of the dog's howling. He knew a dog did not make that kind of noise unless it was hurting, frightened, or both. Once Buddy had stepped on a thorn that had gone deep into his paw. He had whimpered and howled with every step he took until Dad had found the thorn and removed it. Charles had never forgotten that.

"The sound must be coming from that settlement to the East," said Sammy, pointing to a distant row of houses whose roofs barely showed through the thick, tall woods. Obviously, Sammy wasn't ready to quit the expeditioning game. "We'll blaze a trail through the forest and rescue the poor animal. Let's go, men!"

Charles leapt over the stream, stepping quickly from rock to rock with David and Sammy close behind him. He plunged into the woods. There was no path, but he pushed through the undergrowth, ignoring the thorns that caught his sleeves and poked his hands. It seemed even darker in the woods; the trees loomed high above them. Charles felt his heart beating faster. What if they got lost in the forest? David had the compass in his backpack, but none of them actually knew how to use it. Then Charles heard the howling again, an urgent screeching sound. "That way!" he said, pointing to the right. "It's coming from that direction." He began to jog, dodging trees and rocks and roots. He didn't even care if David and Sammy were keeping up; he just had to get to that dog.

"Hey, a path!" said David. "Why can't we just go this way?"

Charles turned around. Sure enough, David was right. Charles must have crossed it without seeing it: a well-worn dirt path through the woods. It looked as if people had cut branches and beat back the brambles, probably to make a trail to the stream.

"It's not an expedition if you take a path," Sammy protested.

"We're not explorers anymore," said Charles. "We just have to find that dog." The whining had not stopped, and Charles couldn't stand to hear it for one second longer. He turned onto the path and began to run. His backpack bumped and thumped against his shoulders as he galloped down the trail. The screeching sounds of the dog were closer now; Charles felt sure that they were going in the right direction.

Suddenly, the three boys popped out into the open. They were in a yard, like any other yard: There was a swing set and a shed and a vegetable garden with a fence around it.

"The settlement!" said Sammy.

"It's just Maple Street," said David.

Charles didn't care whether it was a settlement or a regular neighborhood. He just wanted to find that dog. "This way," he said after listening for a moment. He cut across the yard they were in, then across three others. One had a pool; one had a rock garden; and one had long grass that needed to be mowed. Each yard brought them closer to the crying dog.

"There!" Charles said, pointing to a small pale-blue house that sat at the end of the street. He broke into a run.

A line was strung between the house and a shed in the backyard. Attached to the line was a long wire. And attached to that wire was a dog.

It was a puppy, really. Just a tiny pup, black and white, with an adorable squashed-in face and funny bat ears that stood straight up when she spotted Charles. For just a moment, she stopped screeching. Then she started again. She ran up and down, whimpering and crying as she zipped back and forth along her line from the house to the shed.

There was a dusty, dry path beneath the line. Charles did not see a food or water bowl or any place for the dog to get out of the weather, other than the shed — but the door to the shed was closed tight. The house was also closed up tight; it was clear that nobody was home.

"This isn't right," he said. He shook his head. "How could anybody leave such a young puppy alone all day?"

David took off his backpack and dropped it to the ground. He moved slowly toward the pup, holding out his hand. "It's okay," he said softly. "It's okay, little pup."

Lizzie sometimes called David a dog whisperer. He seemed to know just how to talk to dogs and puppies and make them feel safe.

The puppy stopped screeching for a moment. She stopped running up and down. She looked at David, cocking her head.

Can I trust you?

Charles and Sammy took off their backpacks, too. "Poor thing," Sammy said. He finally seemed to have forgotten about being Captain Sam. "What are you doing here all by yourself?" He walked toward the dog. Her ears went back and she took off, zipping up and down her run again.

"Careful," said David. "She's scared."

Charles looked at the blue house again. The shades were drawn and the door was shut tight. Nobody was home.

A distant rumbling came from the heavy gray clouds overhead, and the dog began to whimper again as she raced up and down.

Charles glanced up. Thunderstorms were unusual at this time of year, but he was pretty sure that was thunder. The sky was darker than ever. "What are we going to do?" he asked. "We can't just leave her out here to get soaked in the storm."

17

David knelt and opened his arms. "Come here, little one," he said. The puppy stopped crying and running. Her ears went up. She took three slow, small steps toward David.

Help me, please! I'm so lonely and scared.

"We're going to take her back to my house," said David. "That's what."

CHAPTER THREE

"We can't just take her," said Charles. But even as he said it, he knew that David was right. They couldn't leave her, either. The poor puppy was terrified, and she was so small. Soon she would be soaked and shivering — and alone. "Okay," he said, letting out a big breath. "We'll take her. But how? We don't have a leash or a rope or anything."

"I'll carry her," said David. "I'll put her in my backpack."

"First we have to catch her," said Sammy. The dog had turned away from David as they talked, and now she was dashing up and down again, barking her head off.

Charles felt a raindrop hit his nose. He looked up and felt three more on his face: *splish, splash, sploosh*. There was another roll of thunder, louder this time.

"If one of you can catch on to her wire while she runs past, that'll stop her," said Sammy. "Then I'll just grab her."

"No grabbing!" said David. "We have to be gentle, even if it takes a little longer. Can't you see how scared she is?"

Charles watched the puppy run. Her eyes were huge with fear, and her oversized ears were laid back. She was like some wild creature, terrified of being trapped. "Okay," he said. "But we don't have all day. It's going to start pouring any second now."

"Maybe Sammy's idea about catching that wire

is good," said David. "If I can do it in a way that doesn't scare her, we can keep her a little closer and show her that she can trust us." He inched toward the line, slowly stretched out his hand, and waited until the puppy ran closer. "Got it," he said under his breath.

"Let's all kneel down and be really quiet so she knows we're not going to hurt her," said Charles. The boys sat on the ground, forming a loose circle around the puppy. Her eyes grew even wider and she tried to dash away, but David kept hold of her wire.

"Easy, little one," murmured David. "Easy now. We just want to help."

The raindrops were coming faster, hitting the dusty run and sending up the smell of wet dirt. There was a crash of thunder. The puppy began to shake and whimper, and she backed up against Charles's leg. Charles reached out a hand — slowly,

slowly. He touched her gently. He felt her flinch, then relax as he unhooked the clasp attached to her collar. "I think she's going to let us help," he whispered. He reached out his other hand and cupped her small, trembling body, then pulled her into his chest. She was a tiny thing, as light as a feather.

"Yes!" whispered David.

"Open your backpack," Charles said softly.

Sammy shucked off his sweatshirt. "We can wrap her in this," he said, handing it over.

Soon the puppy was swaddled in the soft green sweatshirt and tucked into David's backpack. David strapped the backpack on backward, so the puppy was in front. All Charles could see were her large, frightened eyes and funny bat ears. "Come on," David said. He turned and started in the opposite direction from the way they had come.

"Wait, where are you going?" Charles had figured they would take the trail back to the stream, then work their way to David's backyard.

"All we have to do is take Maple to Elm," David called over his shoulder as he trotted toward the street.

Charles almost had to laugh, in spite of the storm and the frightened dog. Of course. Their expeditioning had not brought them deep into the wilderness. That part had been just a game. In real life, they were only a few blocks from David's house.

The boys walked out to the street. Charles took one last look back at the blue house, which sat quiet and empty. What would the people think when they came home and found their dog gone? He imagined how he would feel if Buddy suddenly went missing. But did these people care about the black-and-white puppy the way he cared about

Buddy? They couldn't! Not if they left her all alone on that run all day.

Still, it didn't seem right to take the puppy with no explanation. "Wait," he said to David. "We should leave a note, at least, with your family's phone number on it." Charles pulled off his back-pack and rummaged around for the expedition log and a pencil. He tore out a page and scrawled a quick note on it — *Your dog was scared of the storm, so we took her home* — then added the phone number David told him.

Thunder boomed and the rain kept falling. The drops were big and cold, and they came down hard. "Go on," Charles said. "I'll catch up." He sprinted back to the blue house and stuck the note between the screen door and the front door, then sprinted even faster to catch up with David and Sammy. His sneakers squished as he ran, and his backpack bumped loosely around behind him. He'd been in too much of a hurry to tighten the straps.

He caught up to his friends and they all ran together without talking. Charles's heart was pounding as they rounded the corner onto Elm. There was David's house at the end of the block. Just before they got to it, David stopped. "Wait," he said. "Let's take her straight through the basement door. That will give us some time."

"Time for what?" asked Sammy.

"Time to think about what we're going to do next," David said, looking down at the puppy strapped to his chest. She had snuggled down into the backpack. All that showed were those funny bat ears that looked like they belonged to a much bigger dog. She poked her head up a little further. Her big triangular ears swiveled this way and that as she sniffed the air.

Where are we now? What's going to happen next?

Charles felt his stomach flip over as he looked at the tiny dog's adorable black-and-white face. He and his friends had just done something so wrong — and at the same time, so very right. How could that be?

CHAPTER FOUR

They went around the side of David's house, and Sammy and Charles each took hold of a handle on the big metal doors that covered the steps into the basement. "Ready, Captain?" said Charles. "Heave ho!" They pulled with all their strength and the heavy doors opened.

David disappeared down the steps, then called softly back, "It's okay. The inside door is unlocked. Come on down."

"Should we close the big doors?" Charles asked once they were all on the steps.

David shook his head. "They're too heavy. I'll

tell my dad in a few minutes. Let's just get this puppy settled in."

It was a relief to get out of the pounding rain. Unlike the Petersons' basement, which was damp and dark and had a clanky furnace, David's basement was warm and dry. It was set up as a home gym, with all sorts of equipment arranged on cushy blue mats. David took off the backpack and set it gently on the floor, then stripped off his soaking jacket and hung it on a stationary bicycle. Charles took off his wet jacket, too. He spread his out over the rowing machine. Sammy, in a dripping T-shirt, hugged his arms to his chest. "I need my sweatshirt back," he said. "I'm freezing. Get that puppy out of your backpack."

"In a minute. Let's sit down again so we don't scare her," said David. "Then I'll take her out and she can explore."

Again, they formed a loose circle, with the

backpack in the middle. David opened the top of his backpack and pushed it down a little so the puppy could easily see out. She stared at each of the boys in turn. Her big black eyes were still wide with fear, but first one ear, then the other, stood up straight as she looked around. Then both ears swiveled this way and that, as if they were picking up some sort of signal.

What's going on? Where am I?

She did not even try to climb out of the backpack, and when David leaned forward to push it open a little more, she squinched down inside it and peeped out with glistening eyes.

"I guess she needs some time to get used to everything," Sammy said, sounding a bit disappointed. "I thought she'd be happy just to be inside."

"She's even more shy than Slinky," said Charles.

"Slinky!" David put his hand over his mouth. "Uh-oh. I hope she's not down here. She has been hanging around in the basement lately. She has a little bed made out of old towels, near the furnace." He made a *psst, psst* noise. "Slinky? Are you here?"

There was a rustle from a corner of the basement, and Slinky appeared, stretching and yawning. She was a pretty cat, a tortoiseshell with a shiny, short coat in shades of brown, black, and white.

"Watch, she'll run off as soon as she sees that there's something in the backpack," said David.

But she didn't. Instead, Slinky moved closer, sniffing the air as she approached the circle the boys had made. She seemed more curious than afraid. As the cat got closer to the backpack, the puppy ducked even deeper inside so that only the tippy-tips of her bat ears showed.

"Wow!" said David. "That's a first. Somebody is more afraid of Slinky than Slinky is of them." He reached out his hand and Slinky moved over to rub against him. She was never shy of David. "I'd better take the cat upstairs and at least tell my parents that we're here. I don't want my mom to freak out about me being caught in that storm."

He stood up and gathered Slinky into his arms. He listened at the bottom of the stairs. "They're not arguing anymore, at least," he said. "You guys see if you can get the puppy to come out. I'll be right back." He headed up the inside stairs.

Charles and Sammy sat quietly, watching the backpack for any signs of movement. After a long pause the puppy pushed her head out, like a turtle poking out of its shell. "Hi, puppy," said Charles, slowly putting out his hand. "Hi, little girl."

She pushed out a little further, looking around and sniffing as if to make sure the terrifying creature was gone. Her big eyes and huge swiveling bat ears made her look so cute and funny Charles almost burst out laughing, but he held it in. He didn't want to scare her.

"Good girl," he said softly. He held out his hand a little further, and the puppy slipped all the way out of the backpack and inched her way toward him. Her flat little face wriggled as she sniffed and snuffled, closer and closer. Finally, she bumped her nose right into his hand, and when Charles gave her cheek a gentle scratch, she seemed to relax against his touch.

Sammy reached for the backpack and pulled out his sweatshirt. He pulled off his wet shirt and shrugged into the dry one. "Ahh, much better," he said. He sniffed the sleeve. "It even smells like puppy. Yum."

"Hey," said Charles. "There's a tag on her collar. Maybe we can find out her name." Charles put out his other hand and carefully scooped the puppy toward him, pulling her onto his lap for a cuddle. "See?" he said. "I'm not going to hurt you." He checked the red heart-shaped tag that dangled from her pink collar. "I'm not going to hurt you, Lola."

"Lola," said Sammy. "I like it."

Just then, the door upstairs opened and David trudged down the stairs. Behind him was his father, looking very serious. Charles pulled Lola closer and tried to hide her in his shirt. Sammy jumped up and put himself between Charles and the stairs, with a "Puppy? What puppy?" look plastered on his face.

"It's okay," David said. "Dad knows everything. Lola's owner already called."

CHAPTER FIVE

David's dad shook his head as he walked down the stairs. "Boys, boys," he said, "what were you thinking?"

"I told you, Dad," said David. "She was so scared. She would have gotten soaked if we didn't take her. She could have even gotten hit by lightning or something. We might have saved her life!"

David's father's face softened when he spotted the puppy. "Oh, she's just a little thing," he said.

"That's what I've been trying to tell you," said David.

"Still," said his dad, "we can't just go around taking people's animals. Lucky for you, the owner didn't sound too mad when he called. He said he was just happy to know that she was safe."

When he heard that, Charles was glad that he had left the note. "So what now?" he asked. "Does he want her back?"

"He wants us to come over with her," said David's dad. "I have a funny feeling that he may be looking for a new home for — what's her name again?"

"Lola," said Charles. His heart was thumping in his chest. Was Lola about to become his family's next foster puppy? How great would that be? He was already a little bit in love with the funny bat-eared pup. She was timid, but he knew what to do about that. He remembered when his family had fostered another frightened puppy. Moose was a Great Dane, a gentle giant who was afraid of his own shadow. Charles had helped Moose, and he was sure he could help Lola, too.

"I'm pretty sure my family would foster her," said Charles. "Maybe I should even call my mom and ask her before we go see Lola's owner — just to be sure."

"Good idea," said David's dad. He dug into his pocket and pulled out his phone. "Trade you," he said. He handed over the phone, and Charles let him take Lola.

While Charles was on the phone with his mom, explaining the whole story, David and his dad and Sammy sat down on the blue mat and let Lola explore. She must have been feeling a tiny bit bolder. As Charles talked and watched, she walked around inside the circle they made, snuffling and sniffing. Once, when she was sniffing David's hand, Charles even saw her wagging her stumpy tail.

"So can I tell her owner that we'll help Lola?" Charles finally asked his mom. She had not been happy to hear that he and his friends had taken someone's dog, and she had interrupted his story more than a few times to let him know it.

She sighed, but Charles knew what that sigh meant. It meant "yes," as long as Dad agreed. And Dad always agreed. Charles grinned and told her he'd call her back as soon as he knew more. Then he gave his friends a thumbs-up. "We can take her," he said.

"Not so fast," said David's father. He gathered Lola into his arms and stood up. "First we have to go talk to her owner."

Outside, the storm was over but the sky was still filled with low, dark clouds. They piled into David's parents' tiny red car. David held Lola in his lap as his dad drove back to the blue house on Maple Street. It didn't look so empty now: some of the curtains were open, and a white truck was parked in the driveway outside the garage.

"'Reliable Rod's Plumbing and Heating,'" Charles read from the side of the truck. "'Twenty-four-hour service.'" He knew what "reliable" meant: that this plumber was somebody you could count on. He wasn't sure that this Rod was so reliable when it came to dogs.

"He must be a busy man," said David's dad. "Plumbers are always on the run, helping people with emergencies." They walked up to the house and knocked on the door. "Lola!" said the man who opened it. David placed Lola gently into his hands. "I'm so sorry, baby girl," the man murmured as he hugged the little dog to his chest. For a moment, they all just stood quietly. Then the man seemed to remember that there were other people there. "Come in, come in," he said. "I'm Rod Fletcher. Thank you for getting Lola out of that storm."

David's dad shook hands with Rod, then intro-duced all three boys. "They didn't mean to scare you by taking her," he said. "They were just wor-ried about the pup."

Rod nodded. "I worry about her, too. My wife and I got her a few months ago, and we are just over the moon for her. I mean, look at her. She's such a little sweetie. But my wife is a sergeant in the National Guard, and she got called up to serve. She left for Afghanistan a week ago, and she could be gone for two years."

He seemed to choke up on his last sentence, and he buried his nose in Lola's fur.

"That must be hard," said David's dad.

"It sure is," said Rod. "And one of the hardest parts is figuring out how to deal with Lola. She's always been a timid puppy, but since my wife left it's gotten worse. I can't take her with me on the truck because she's afraid of everything, and if I leave her alone inside, she freaks out. I can't say no when people call me with emergencies, so I've been leaving her out on the run when I take off to fix a broken furnace or leaking pipes." He hung his head. "I know it's not a perfect solution, but I'm not sure what else I can do. I'm just getting my business started up, and I can't afford a dog-sitter or anything like that."

Charles spoke up. "My family fosters puppies," he said. "We can't take her for two whole years, but we can keep her for a while, and help find her a good home if that's what you decide she needs."

Rod was quiet for a few moments. Then he shook his head and let out a long breath. "I don't know," he said.

CHAPTER SIX

"So then what happened?" Mr. Mason leaned forward, eager to hear the rest of the story Charles and his friends were telling. It was Monday morning at school, time for sharing, and everybody was excited about the tale of Lola's rescue.

"Then he said yes," said Charles. "He said my family should take her. He was really sad. I think he might have been crying a little bit." He could still picture the plumber's crumpled face as Rod had looked down at the little dog in his arms.

"What about when his wife gets back?" asked Scarlett, one of the girls in the class.

"He thinks it would be best if they started fresh, with a new puppy," Charles said. "So he wants us to find Lola a new home."

"Me, me, me!" said Lucy, throwing her hand in the air. Lucy was almost as dog-crazy as Lizzie. "Lola sounds so cute."

Mr. Mason laughed. "I think your parents would say you already have enough pets," he reminded her. Lucy and her family had a whole zoo's worth of animals: three dogs, a couple of guinea pigs, a hutch full of bunnies and a coop full of chickens, and even five sheep. She always had a lot of stories to tell at morning meeting, about chickens who laid eggs in funny places, sheep who ate too much and got bellyaches, and guinea pigs who escaped from their cages.

"I don't think Lola's really ready for a new home yet," said Charles. "She's so timid. Lizzie says she probably missed out on getting socialized — that means meeting new people and dogs and going different places. Lizzie says that when a puppy is very young, it should be experiencing dozens of new things every week! If puppies don't do that at the right time, they can become scaredy-dogs, like Lola, or like Moose, that Great Dane my family fostered. Then it takes a lot longer for them to learn to be comfortable with new things."

"Does Lizzie know what kind of dog the new puppy is?" asked Mr. Mason. Everybody in Charles's class knew that Lizzie was an expert on dog breeds.

"She says Lola is a French bulldog," said Charles. "She'll never be really big, but once she gets over being timid, she will probably be a little clown. Lizzie says that's what the breed is known for."

"Well, so far everything seems to be turning out well," said Mr. Mason, checking his watch.

Morning meeting was just about over, and Charles and his story had taken up the whole time. "But I hope you boys aren't going to make a habit of dog-napping people's pets."

"No way," said Sammy.

David shook his head.

"That's what my mom said," Charles told Mr. Mason.

Mr. Mason nodded. "Good. Well, if nobody has anything else urgent to share, it's time to get to work on our projects. Everybody please break up into your groups. We'll have some library time later this morning, so think about any research you'll need to do."

Sammy, Charles, and David pulled their desks together and started to talk about their project. They had a lot of material already, but they still needed to research things like animals of the West, mapmaking, and the customs of the fifty different Native American tribes across the expedition route. They were doing all the research together. Then Charles, who liked writing, would create the written report. David, the best artist, would draw pictures to illustrate it. And Sammy, who loved to stand up in front of an audience and get attention, would do the oral report.

"No jokes," Charles reminded him now. He knew that Sammy could hardly talk for five minutes without telling a silly joke or riddle. "This is serious stuff."

"Maybe just one or two good ones," Sammy said. "My dad says jokes are how you keep an audience interested."

Charles and David looked at each other, shrugged, and rolled their eyes. Sammy was going to put jokes in no matter what they said.

Mr. Mason stopped by their desks. "How's it going?" he asked. "Do you need to go to the library?" Mr. Mason liked them to use the library as well as the computers. He said it was good for them to know how to do both kinds of research.

Charles nodded. He showed Mr. Mason his notebook, already filling up with information. "I'm doing the writing part," he said.

Mr. Mason shook his head. "Nope," he said.

"What?" asked Charles.

"Since this unit is on explorers, I want all of you to explore some new areas of learning, too," said Mr. Mason. "I don't want any of you doing what you're best at. That's why I want you to do the artwork for your team's report, Charles."

Charles blinked. "But I can't draw," he said. "My dogs look like hippos and my people look like trees."

Mr. Mason shrugged. "I'm sure you'll figure out a good way to illustrate the report," he said, "which, by the way, Sammy will be writing."

Sammy's eyebrows shot up. "Me?" he squeaked. "Writing?"

Charles knew that Sammy avoided writing whenever possible. His spelling was terrible, his handwriting was unreadable, and he did not understand anything about punctuation.

"Yes, you," said Mr. Mason. "And as for you, David . . ."

David was shaking his head. "No! Don't make me do it," he begged.

"Yes, you will deliver the oral report," Mr. Mason finished.

David groaned and put his head down on the desk.

When Charles had first met David, he was almost as shy as Slinky. He'd gotten better, but he still hated talking in front of anyone other than Charles and Sammy. When Mr. Mason called on him in class, he always turned bright red and had a hard time getting the words out of his mouth, even if it was something simple, like the answer to a math problem (David was a math wizard) or the right way to spell a word (he always got a hundred on his spelling tests).

Mr. Mason patted David on the back. "You'll all do fine," he said. "Remember, you're brave explorers, going places you've never gone before." He walked off, smiling.

"We're dead," said Sammy.

"This is a disaster," said Charles.

David didn't even lift his head from the desk. He just groaned again.

CHAPTER SEVEN

"We're dead," Sammy said again later that afternoon. The friends were at the Petersons' house. They had gone there after school to work on their report. They all had wanted to see Lola again, for one thing. For another, the Petersons' big dining room table was the best place to spread out and work.

Sammy threw down his pencil. "I've already erased that word five times," he said. "There's just a big hole in the paper. How do you spell 'expedition,' anyway?"

Charles sighed. "I can spell it, but I sure can't illustrate it." He pointed to his paper, where he'd been trying to draw a picture of Lewis and Clark paddling their loaded keelboat up the Missouri River. It looked like something the Bean might have drawn.

"It doesn't even matter," said David. "We're all going to flunk anyway, because I'm not going to be able to open my mouth on Friday. A ten-minute report in front of the whole class? I can't believe he's making me do it." Once again, he put his head down on the table and groaned. "Save me, Lola," he said. Then he giggled. "No, Lola! I didn't say 'lick my ears.' I said 'save me.'" Lola wagged her tail and licked some more.

Oops, sorry. Your ears are just too delicious.

Lola snuggled in David's lap. She seemed to feel safe there, even though Charles's mom told them that she had been very timid all day.

"She wouldn't sit on my lap that way," Mom said when she saw how Lola went to David. "She's afraid of the vacuum cleaner, she's afraid of the Bean, she's afraid of Buddy, she's afraid of his toys . . ." She ticked off one finger at a time as she listed the tiny puppy's fears. "I tried to be as gentle and quiet with her as I could, but she just can't seem to settle in here. Dad took Buddy down to the firehouse for the day, just to give her more space, but she's still acting very skittish." Then she said something that made a chill go down Charles's spine. "You know, if she can't adjust to our household, we may have to call Ms. Dobbins."

"No!" said Charles. Not that there was anything wrong with Ms. Dobbins. She was a very nice person. It was just that she was the director of the local animal shelter. There was nothing wrong with Caring Paws, either. It was a wonderful place for the dogs and cats who ended up there, but it would not be a wonderful place for a tiny, timid puppy like Lola.

Mom had shrugged. "We'll see," she'd said.

She went into the kitchen and came back through the dining room with a mug of coffee in her hand. She was headed to her upstairs office. As a newspaper reporter, Charles's mom did a lot of work from home. "Well, Lola seems happy enough now," she said, smiling at the bat ears, whose tips just showed above the table. "But you boys don't. What's the matter?"

Charles explained. "Mr. Mason unveiled his diabolical plan today," he said. "He's making us all do things we hate to do or just plain can't do." He pulled back so his mom could see the drawing he was working on.

"Is that a hippopotamus?" Mom asked, turning her head sideways. "I thought you were doing

Lewis and Clark on the Missouri River, not Stanley and Livingston in Africa."

Charles sat back with a sigh. "See?" he asked his friends. "Even my mom says I'm a terrible artist."

"That's not what I —" Mom began.

"My mom would say the same about my writing," said Sammy.

"And my parents know I can't stand to talk in public," David added.

"But you're all such smart and talented boys," Mom said. "I think Mr. Mason is right. If you'll just explore a little, you can figure out how to make this report fantastic."

She told them about how sometimes, when she was writing an article for the paper, she had no idea how to get started. "Then I just start playing around," she said. "I try one way, or I try another.

Sometimes I start at the end and circle back to the beginning, or I even begin right in the middle. Sometimes I just stop writing and do some yoga instead. Then, when I'm in the middle of a headstand, a great idea will pop into my brain."

Immediately, Sammy got out of his chair and tried to do a headstand. His feet banged against the dining room wall and three pictures went crooked. "It's not helping," he said in a funny upside-down voice.

David and Charles got down on the floor, too. Lola licked David's face as he and Charles tried to stand on their heads next to Sammy.

Mom laughed. "I didn't necessarily mean that you should all stand on your heads," she said. "I'm just suggesting that you should try thinking outside the box, as they say." She picked up her coffee mug and headed upstairs. "Good luck," she said over her shoulder as all three boys thumped back down onto the floor.

They lay there for a moment, panting. Why was it such hard work to stand on your head?

"Okay," said Sammy. "I'm thinking outside the box. Mr. Mason didn't say the report had to be handwritten, did he? If I can type it on my dad's computer, I can use spelling and grammar check, and nobody will have to read my handwriting."

Charles rolled over and gave his friend a high five. "Great idea," he said. "And I'm thinking outside the box, too. What if I trace one of the maps we've found, of Lewis and Clark's expedition, and then blow it up bigger? I can make a time line along the bottom and just put in a few little symbols to show trees or mountains or rivers. I won't really have to draw, but it will still be an illustration." Suddenly, he was itching to get to work. He could see the whole map in his imagination. It would be fantastic.

"Wow, those headstands worked," said David, rubbing his head. "I had a brainstorm, too. I think Lola should come and stay with my family."

"What?" Charles stared at his friend.

David shrugged. "Why not? There's so much going on here, but our house is pretty quiet. Plus, Lola seems to kind of like me." He blushed. "I know we're not an official foster family like you, but I think we could handle one little puppy."

Charles nodded slowly. What David had said made a lot of sense. "Do you think your parents will agree?" he asked.

David nodded. "My dad is already crazy about her. He'll talk Mom into it, as long as I promise to do most of the work and keep Lola and Slinky separated."

Sammy spoke up. "Sounds great . . . except for one thing. Where's Lola?"

Charles glanced around the room. Sure enough, there was no sign of the little black-and-white puppy.

CHAPTER EIGHT

"She must have gotten scared when we were all thumping down from our headstands," said Charles. He stood up and headed for the living room, calling for Lola. "Hmmm," he said. "She's not in here."

"Not here, either," said Sammy, who had gone to check the front hall. "Come out, come out wherever you are," he said.

"Lola," David called softly. "Where are you, baby girl?"

Charles remembered Lola's owner calling her that. Maybe she would come when she heard someone calling her pet name.

But there was no movement, no scampering pup.

Charles went to the kitchen. "Lola?" he called. "Are you in here?" So far, Lola had seemed afraid of the kitchen and had mostly stayed out of that noisy, busy room. Charles had even fed her outside, on the deck, where it was quieter. *The deck!* He went to the sliding doors that led outside. "The door is a little bit open," he said. "She must have run out to the backyard. Good thing there's a fence."

The boys went out onto the deck. No Lola. They walked around the yard, checking under the rosebushes and behind the new compost bin Mom had just put in. No black-and-white puppy. "Where could she have gone?" asked Charles after he'd made sure the gate was closed and locked. Lola was such a tiny girl; he hated to think of her wandering around in the big world all by herself.

"Maybe she didn't come out here after all," said David. "I'm going back inside to look."

Sammy and Charles took one more loop around the backyard, double-checking all the places they had already checked. "She's outta here," said Sammy. "That puppy just, like, disappeared."

Charles felt a knot in his stomach. His family was usually so responsible, but this was not the first time they had lost a foster puppy. He remembered Ziggy, the little dachshund who had been a real escape artist. He'd disappeared, too, and Charles had searched for him for days. Finally, they had found Ziggy, but it had not been easy.

There was a shout from the deck. "Got her!" Charles looked up to see David cradling Lola in his arms. Charles grinned. What a relief.

"Where was she?" Charles asked after he'd bounded up the stairs to pet Lola.

"Under the couch," David said. "Just like Slinky. She didn't want to come out when we were all making a fuss. I sat very still and called her, and after a minute there she was." He buried his face in Lola's fur. "See? She really does need a quieter place to live."

Lola snuggled into David's arms, then stretched out her neck to give him a kiss on the cheek.

I feel so safe with you.

Charles felt a twinge of jealousy. Why did Lola like David best? He wished the puppy would snuggle that way in his arms. Still, the main thing was for Lola to be happy. "I guess you're right," he said.

An hour later, the boys and Lola were over at David's house. "I moved Slinky's bed out of the basement," said David's dad, "so you can hang out down there." He seemed really happy to see Lola. "Hey there, baby girl," he said, petting her tiny head. His voice was as soft as David's. "I'm glad you're going to stay with us for a while."

Charles had brought all his mapmaking supplies along, and now he spread them out on a section of blue mat: tracing paper, colored pencils, an eraser, extra paper. While Sammy and David played with Lola, Charles carefully traced Lewis and Clark's route from a book the boys had been using for research. There was the Missouri River. There were the Great Falls, the Rocky Mountains, the valleys, the Bitterroot Mountains, where the expedition had almost starved, the long trek up the Clearwater, Snake, and Columbia Rivers, and finally the Pacific Ocean. What an amazing journey. Drawing it all, step by step, made it seem more real.

Sammy came to look over his shoulder. "Cool," he said. "We should make a map like that of our own expedition." He sprawled next to Charles on the floor, grabbed a piece of paper, and started to draw. "We went up the creek this way," he said, "then, when we heard Lola crying, we took off into the woods, toward the settlement." His pencil scritched and scratched as he drew. Attracted by the sound, Lola came to investigate. She sniffed her way toward Sammy, her eyes glued to the movements of his pencil.

What's going on over here? I'm so curious.

"Wow, she's getting braver already," said Sammy as Lola moved closer. He stopped scribbling and slowly held out his hand for Lola to sniff. She sat back on her tiny butt and let Sammy pet her head. Her big bat ears rose and fell as he scratched between them. "I think you were right, David. I think she likes it here."

Charles agreed. "Maybe your family should be fostering puppies, too," he said to David.

David looked down at his hands. "Maybe," he said. "If we stay a family."

Charles and Sammy were quiet for a moment. "Your parents are still fighting?" Sammy finally asked.

David shook his head. "No, not really. I even caught them kissing in the kitchen this morning." He made a face. "But something still feels weird. There's something they're not telling me." He shrugged. "It's okay," he said. "Let's see these maps."

Charles turned his drawing so that David could see it, and all three boys pored over the maps. Lola had positioned herself right smack in the middle of everything, lying down on the sweater

Charles had taken off. He had to admit that the little pup seemed much happier and more comfortable at David's house. He was just about to say so when Lola leapt to her feet and charged toward the stairs. "What —" Charles began.

Then he saw that Slinky was there, slipping downstairs to look for her cozy bed by the furnace. The cat took one look at the puppy running toward her and turned tail. Slinky was up the stairs in no time, and Lola pranced back toward Charles and his friends with a smug look on her face.

Yeah, maybe I was once afraid of cats. But not anymore.

Lola threw herself down on the mat and rolled over, asking David for a victory tummy rub.

"What a little clown," said Charles. "Her personality is really starting to come out."

"She's a nut," agreed Sammy.

"That's my brave girl," David said, petting Lola. He looked at the other two. "If she can face down Slinky, I guess I can face down the class while I give an oral report. We're going to ace this thing!" He held up both hands for a group high five, and Sammy and Charles smacked his palms and cheered.

CHAPTER NINE

"Let's see how it came out," Sammy said, pointing to the rolled-up map Charles had carried carefully to school.

It was Friday, report day. Instead of playing kickball outside until the first bell rang, everybody was in Mr. Mason's room, putting final touches on their reports. The classroom was buzzing with excitement.

"Shouldn't we wait for David?" Charles asked.

"He'll be here any minute," said Sammy. "C'mon. Let's see."

Charles unrolled the big map across their desks. He was proud of it. Mom had taken him down to the newspaper office and helped him make a huge blowup of the expedition map he'd drawn. Now that it was big, it looked really professional — almost like something you would see in a museum.

"Wow," said Sammy. "This is so cool." He traced the expedition route with his finger. "It shows everything." He grinned at Charles. "Not bad for somebody who says he can't draw."

Charles smiled back. "Let's see the report," he said.

Sammy unzipped his backpack and pulled out a red folder. "My dad helped me do fancy lettering for the front," he said.

"Nice," said Charles. The report looked very official, with its title, *Lewis and Clark: The Corps of Discovery*, all printed out in big block letters. Charles opened it and read the first paragraph to himself. "This is great," he said when he was done. "And everything is even spelled right, too."

Sammy blushed. "Thanks," he said. "Spell-check. Plus, my mom helped a little with punctuation."

"We are so set," said Charles, giving Sammy a fist bump. "And David's going to do great, too."

"Hmmm," said Sammy, looking past Charles's shoulder to the back of the classroom. "I'm not so sure about that. He doesn't look too happy this morning."

Charles turned to see David approaching their desks. He trudged along with his shoulders hunched over and a worried frown on his face.

"Hey, David," said Charles. "Don't look so serious. You're going to be fine. It's only a little oral report."

David shrugged. "It's not the report I'm worried about," he said. "It's this." He tossed something down on the desk. It looked like a road map, the folded-up kind. "Lola must have been bored this morning while I was eating breakfast. She found this and started to destroy it. I grabbed it from her before it was totally ruined."

Charles noticed the shredded corners. "Are you worried about Lola being destructive?" he asked. "Because we've fostered puppies like that before. Remember Daisy?" Charles shook his head, smiling. Daisy, a Boston terrier the Petersons had fostered, had loved destroying things: couch cushions, toys, anything she came across.

David shook his head. "It's not that."

"What is it, then?" Sammy asked.

David opened the map out and laid it across their desks. It showed the whole United States. There was a route outlined in yellow highlighter. It went from Littleton all the way west to Missoula, Montana. "This explains everything," he said.

Charles shook his head. "I don't get it."

"My dad is always talking about when he used to live out West, when he was a ski bum in Idaho," said David. "He loved it out there and he always wanted to go back, but my mom likes it here."

"Yeah?" Sammy asked. "So?"

"So I think he's moving back out West." David brushed the map off the desk and they all watched it drift to the floor. "Without me and my mom."

Charles didn't know what to say. Sammy didn't seem to, either.

"Boys?" Mr. Mason stopped by their desks. "Everything okay here? All ready for report day?"

"Ready!" said Sammy and Charles.

Mr. Mason was looking at David. "David?" he asked gently.

David just nodded. "Ready," he said. He was staring at the floor.

"Okay, then," said Mr. Mason. He held out an

upside-down baseball cap filled with little squares of paper. "Pick a number to see when you'll give your report."

Charles reached into the hat and picked out a piece of paper. He unfolded it with David and Sammy looking over his shoulder. They all groaned when they saw the number on it. "We're going first," Charles said.

"That's not so bad," said Mr. Mason. "You'll get it over with and then you can just sit back and enjoy all the other reports." He picked up Charles's map. "I'll take this beautiful map and hang it up on the wall for everyone to see," he said.

As Mr. Mason walked away, David plopped down on his chair and let out a big sigh.

Charles picked up the road map on the floor, and he and Sammy sat down, too. "Don't worry," said Charles as he folded up the map. "It's probably not what you think."

"Just focus on the report for now," said Sammy. "Remember how Lola faced down Slinky? You can do it!"

David nodded. "I can do it," he repeated.

"And remember, we're celebrating tonight, explorer-style," said Sammy. The boys had planned a sleepover at David's. They would eat and sleep outdoors, like Lewis and Clark. David's dad had already helped him set up their tent.

"Yeah!" said Charles.

"Yeah," said David, a little less enthusiastically.

Charles wondered. Could David be right about his father leaving? If the worst was true, maybe something good could come out of it. Maybe David's parents would decide that a puppy was the perfect distraction for him. Maybe they would decide to let David keep Lola — forever.

73

CHAPTER TEN

"This is a fine feast, Captain David," Sammy said as he reached for another hot dog. "The cooks on this expedition are the best."

"I agree, Captain Sam," said David. He slathered his hot dog with mustard, ketchup, and relish. "A fine feast for a fine celebration. Right, Captain Charles?"

"Right!" said Charles. He held up his own hot dog, keeping it out of Lola's reach. She sat next to him on the bench of the picnic table. She wagged her little tail and swiveled her bat ears, trying to look her cutest.

Just one bite? Please?

It was Friday night, and the explorers were in David's backyard. The late fall air was crisp; not exactly picnic weather, but the boys were sticking to their plan of eating outdoors. They were still planning to camp, too. Their sleeping bags were already laid out inside the tent.

David's mom had bought all the provisions, and David's dad had made a roaring bonfire in the fire pit so that they could roast their hot dogs and marshmallows. Of course, Lewis and Clark would not have had hot dogs and marshmallows, so the boys were pretending to eat bison steaks and wild cattails.

"You really nailed that oral report, David," said Sammy, for the tenth time. "Mr. Mason was smiling the whole time."

"I think he liked the jokes that you put in," said David. "So did everybody else."

"And your map looked great hanging up on the board," Sammy said to Charles.

Their report on Lewis and Clark had been everyone's favorite — and it wasn't just the surprise of David standing up in front of the class and telling jokes. It was also the map Charles had made and the way Sammy had put together all the information they had gathered.

"Are we still going to do expeditioning?" Sammy asked. "I mean, now that the report is done."

"Definitely," said David. "I'm in, as long as Lola can come. She loves to explore, too, now that she's not so scared all the time."

When Lola heard her name, she jumped up onto the table and started to prance around, showing off.

The boys laughed, and David scooped the tiny puppy into his arms to give her a hug. Lola's little pink tongue darted out to lick David's cheek, and he laughed some more.

Charles felt a twinge. He wondered how long his friend's good mood would last once he knew the truth. David's dad really was leaving! Charles had heard it for himself. Just before dinner, Charles had gone into David's house to use the bathroom. He hadn't meant to eavesdrop, but he'd heard David's parents talking in the kitchen. "The van will be here in the morning," David's dad had said.

That could mean only one thing: a moving van.

Charles couldn't stand to tell David what he'd heard. His friend would know soon enough.

Meanwhile, even though he'd managed to swallow only a few bites of hot dog, Charles's stomach was twisting and rumbling. He put his hand on his belly. "My stomach really hurts," he said. "I think I might be getting sick."

"Do you still want to camp out?" David asked.

Charles shook his head. "I don't think so," he said. "I think I want to go home." Suddenly, he really did want to be home, sleeping in his own bed. He definitely did not want to be at David's house when that moving van arrived.

That was the end of the sleepover. After David's mom called Charles's mom, she suggested that the boys reschedule their campout for the next night. "As long as everyone's feeling okay," she said.

Charles wondered about that as he sat next to Sammy in the backseat on the drive home. How could David ever feel okay on the day his father moved out?

"Charles, David is on the phone." Charles woke with a start the next morning when he heard his mom calling.

He felt a lump in his stomach. Had the moving van already arrived? David must be phoning to tell him about it.

"Can you and Sammy come right over?" David asked when Charles answered. He didn't sound upset. Actually, he sounded excited.

"Um, sure," said Charles. "Is — is everything okay?"

"My parents gave me a big surprise this morning. You'll see," said David. Then he hung up without another word.

Charles asked his mom if she could drive him and Sammy to David's. He called Sammy, then pulled on his jeans and a sweatshirt. By the time he was dressed, Sammy was already in the kitchen, wolfing down a piece of toast spread with peanut butter. Mom handed one to Charles, too. "Ready?" she asked.

The van was the first thing Charles saw when they pulled up in front of David's. But it wasn't a big moving truck. It was just an oversized van, sparkling new and bright blue, with windows all around.

"Cool," said Mom. "When did David's family get a camper van?"

David ran out of the house. "Look what we got!" he said as Charles and Sammy piled out of the car. "My family's going exploring." He pulled open the sliding door of the blue van and the boys peered inside.

"First my dad has to get it all set up, with beds and cabinets and a kitchen," said David. "That's going to be his job for the next few months. But when summer vacation comes, we're hitting the road. Westward ho!" He was beaming. "We might even follow some of Lewis and Clark's route."

"That's really cool. But . . . are you coming back?" Charles asked.

David looked more serious as he pulled the van door shut. "Well, my parents say that depends on what we find while we explore. If we find a place we all really love, we might stay there for a while. You know how my dad has always wanted to live out West again? If he finds a good job there, my mom says we can try it out. Like for a year or so."

Just then, Lola ran out of the house and began to sniff all around the van.

What's all this? It smells very interesting.

She put her feet up on the side of the van. "She wants to see inside," said David. "She wants to check out her new home."

"New home?" Charles stared at David.

"That's the best part," David said, scooping Lola into his arms. "She's coming with us! Lola is going to be part of our family's Corps of Discovery." He buried his nose in the little dog's neck. "Dad loves her already and Mom says she's the perfect size to fit in our camper van."

"That's awesome!" Charles said. Lucky Lola. She was going on a really big expedition. The little black-and-white pooch was going to have the happiest, most exciting life ever. "I mean, we're really going to miss you, but it sounds like a cool trip."

Sammy nodded and gave David a soft punch in the arm. "Yeah, you better promise to come back, okay?"

"I promise," David said, holding out his pinkie for a special shake. "Corps of Discovery forever!" he said.

"Corps of Discovery forever!" Sammy and Charles shouted.

Lola swiveled her big bat ears and gave a happy little bark.

Let the adventures begin!

PUPPY TIPS

Did Charles and his friends do the right thing when they rescued Lola? We all want to help animals when we see them being mistreated, but there might be better ways to go about it. Things turned out well in Lola's story — but if you see an animal that seems to be neglected, you should not jump in the way they did. The first thing to do is tell an adult: a teacher, a parent, or another relative. The next step would be to alert your local humane society or animal control officer. They will check out the situation and make sure that the animal is safe and is being cared for.

Dear Reader,

Someday I would love to drive around the United States, Canada, and Mexico in a camper van, stopping wherever I want to check out special places, meet people, and see friends. I'm not sure that my dog, Zipper, would enjoy it as much as I would, though. He needs to run every day, and he's a lot bigger than Lola. Maybe when he's a little older and more mellow we will take a long trip together. Meanwhile, I'll start making a list of all the places I want to go!

Yours from the Puppy Place,
Ellen Miles

P.S. For another book about a little dog with a big personality, check out DAISY.

THE PUPPY PLACE
Where every puppy finds a home

DAISY

ELLEN MILES

◼SCHOLASTIC

THE PUPPY PLACE

DON'T MISS THE NEXT PUPPY PLACE ADVENTURE!

Here's a sneak peek at ANGEL!

Ms. Sharma stopped suddenly in the middle of the path and held up her hand to let everyone else know that they should stop, too. She turned her face to the sky. "Spshsh!" She made a funny noise with her mouth. "Spshsh, spshsh!"

"What's she doing?" Lizzie Peterson whispered into her friend Maria's ear. "What is that noise?"

Maria put a finger over her lips, reminding

Lizzie that they were supposed to be on a silent hike. But then she leaned in close to Lizzie's ear and whispered back, "She's calling that bird. See?" She pointed to the crown of a nearby tree. "That noise is like one that birds make to let each other know that danger is near. When she does it, the birds come out to see what's happening. Birdwatchers call it 'spishing.' My dad does it, too."

Lizzie squinted. Way up in the highest branches, she saw a tiny blob that might have been a bird. Yes! It was moving. It was a bird. It flitted down to a lower branch, then flitted again, perching at last on a branch right over their heads. It almost seemed as if the bird was responding to Ms. Sharma's noise.

Lizzie shook her head. It couldn't be. Dogs came when you called — that is, they did if they were properly trained — but not wild birds. Not this little brown bird with white feathers on his chest.

"Spshsh, spshsh," said Ms. Sharma again. Another bird popped out of the leaves, and Lizzie froze in place. So did everyone else in her group.

"Wow," breathed Lizzie. The birds were definitely responding. How cool was that? This moment alone made the whole hike worthwhile. It had not been easy getting up at six a.m. on a Saturday. Finding her hiking boots had been a challenge, too. And the steep, rocky scramble Ms. Sharma had led them on was "no walk in the park," as Lizzie's dad would say.

Except that it was. At least, it was a walk in the Agnes Dimsdale Nature Preserve, which was kind of like a park. Lizzie was there with the Greenies, a new club that had formed at school. It wasn't only for middle grade kids — there were high school students and even a few adults in the club. Their focus was on saving the environment, and Ms. Sharma was the club advisor.

Ms. Sharma was a sixth grade science teacher. Even before Lizzie had met her, she knew that Ms. Sharma was famous for knowing everything about the environment and for being passionate about trying to save it. Ms. Sharma had convinced the school to start composting and growing its own vegetables. She had led a campaign to replace all the plastic forks and knives in the cafeteria with special biodegradable utensils that would melt away into nothing when they were thrown out. And every year she planned a huge fundraiser for the protection of wild tigers.

Lizzie was totally into the idea of helping the environment, especially animals. She loved and wanted to protect animals, all kinds — but especially dogs. Maybe dogs were not in danger of going extinct, like tigers were, but some dogs still needed help. For example, the puppies that Lizzie's family fostered. The Petersons took care of puppies who needed homes, just until they could find each one the perfect home. Lizzie was proud of the work that her family did. It was never easy to give up the puppies when it was time, but it always felt good to know that they were going to safe, loving homes.

ABOUT THE AUTHOR

Ellen Miles loves dogs, which is why she has a great time writing the Puppy Place books. And guess what? She loves cats, too! (In fact, her very first pet was a beautiful tortoiseshell cat named Jenny.) That's why she came up with the Kitty Corner series. Ellen lives in Vermont and loves to be outdoors with her dog, Zipper, every day, walking, biking, skiing, or swimming, depending on the season. She also loves to read, cook, explore her beautiful state, play with dogs, and hang out with friends and family.

Visit Ellen at www.ellenmiles.net.